S0-DJE-498

Having Fun

by Michèle Dufresne

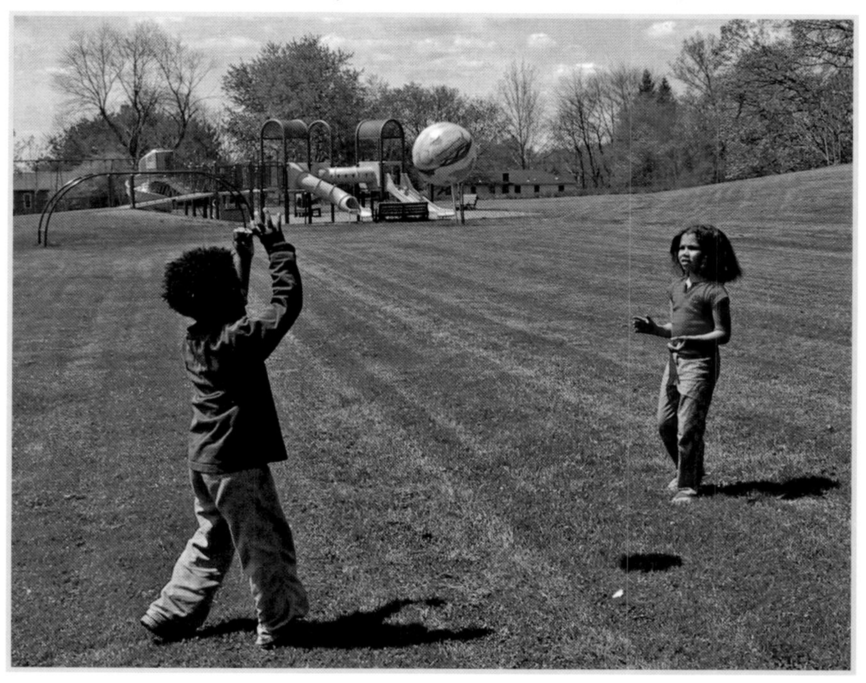

Pioneer Valley Educational Press, Inc.

I like to jump rope.

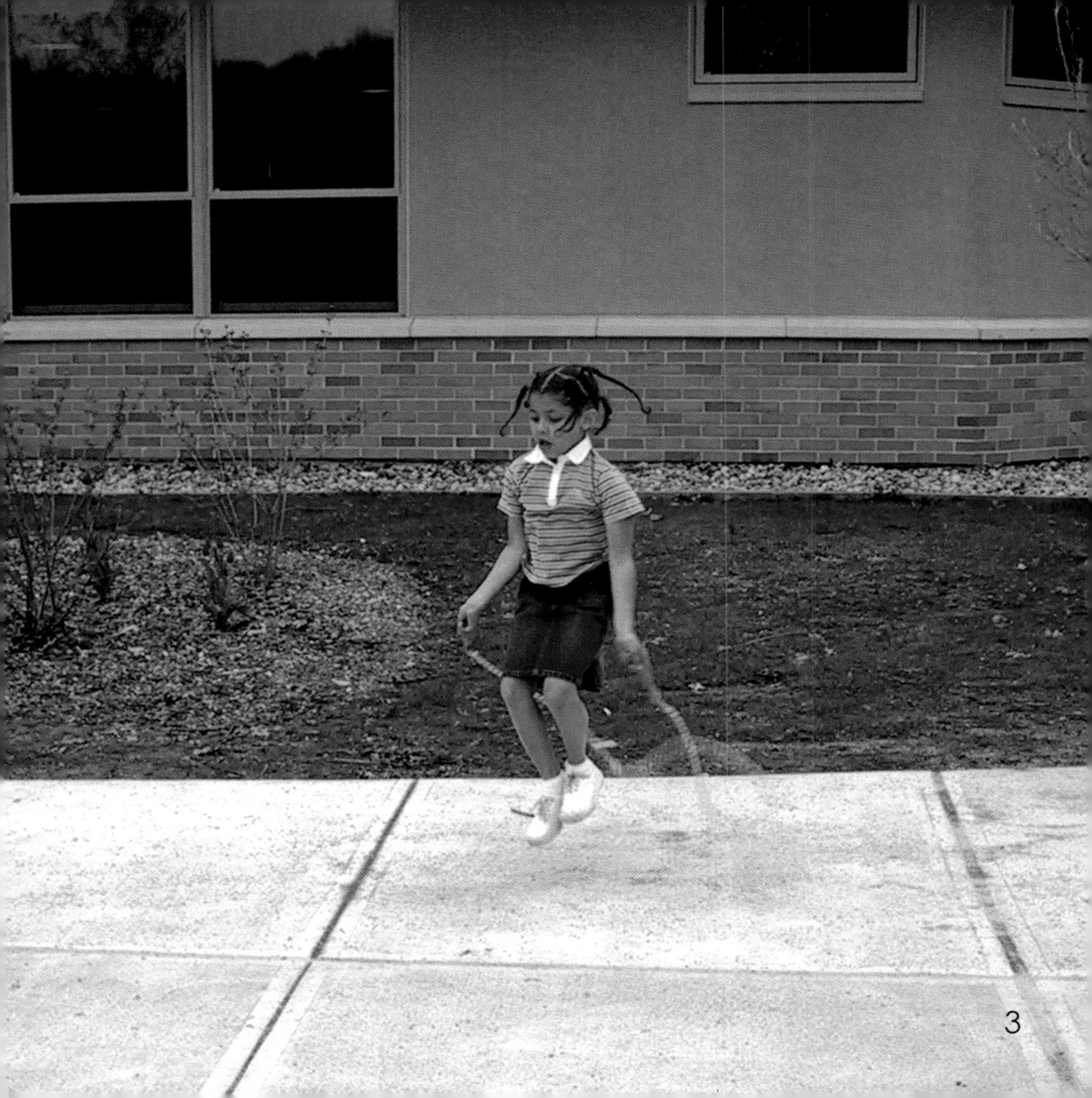

I like to skateboard.

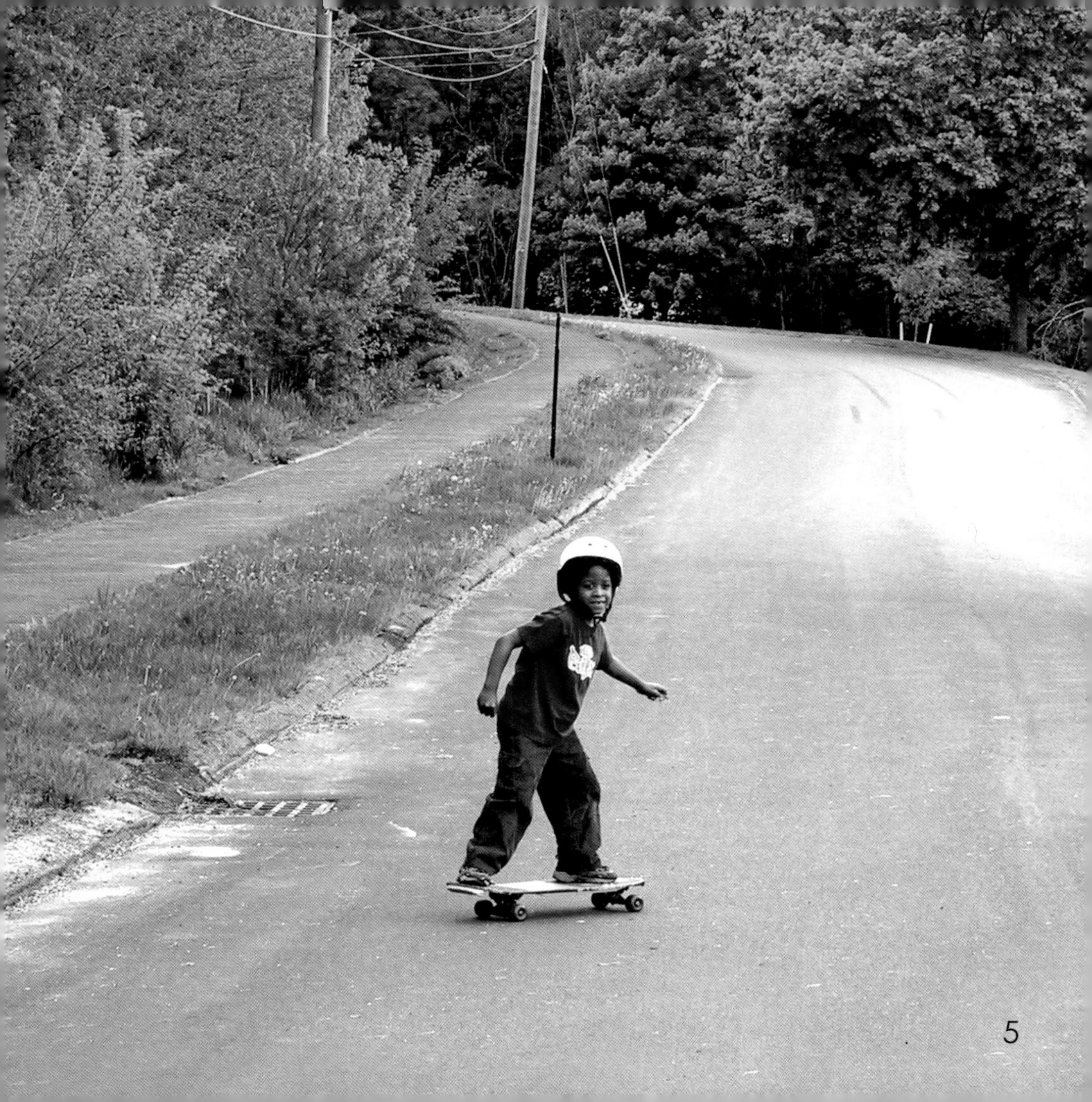

I like to go
down the slide.

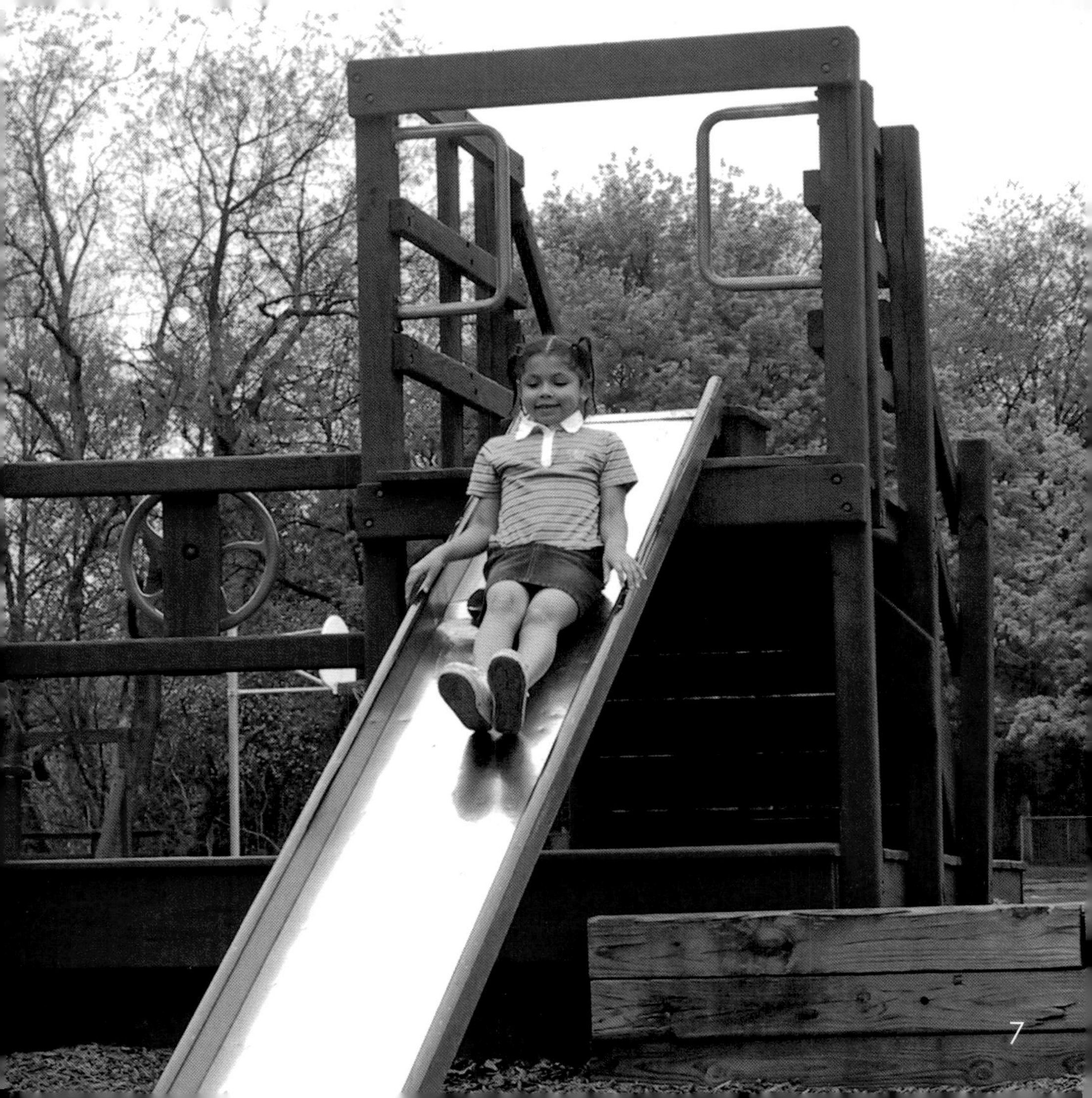

We like to run.

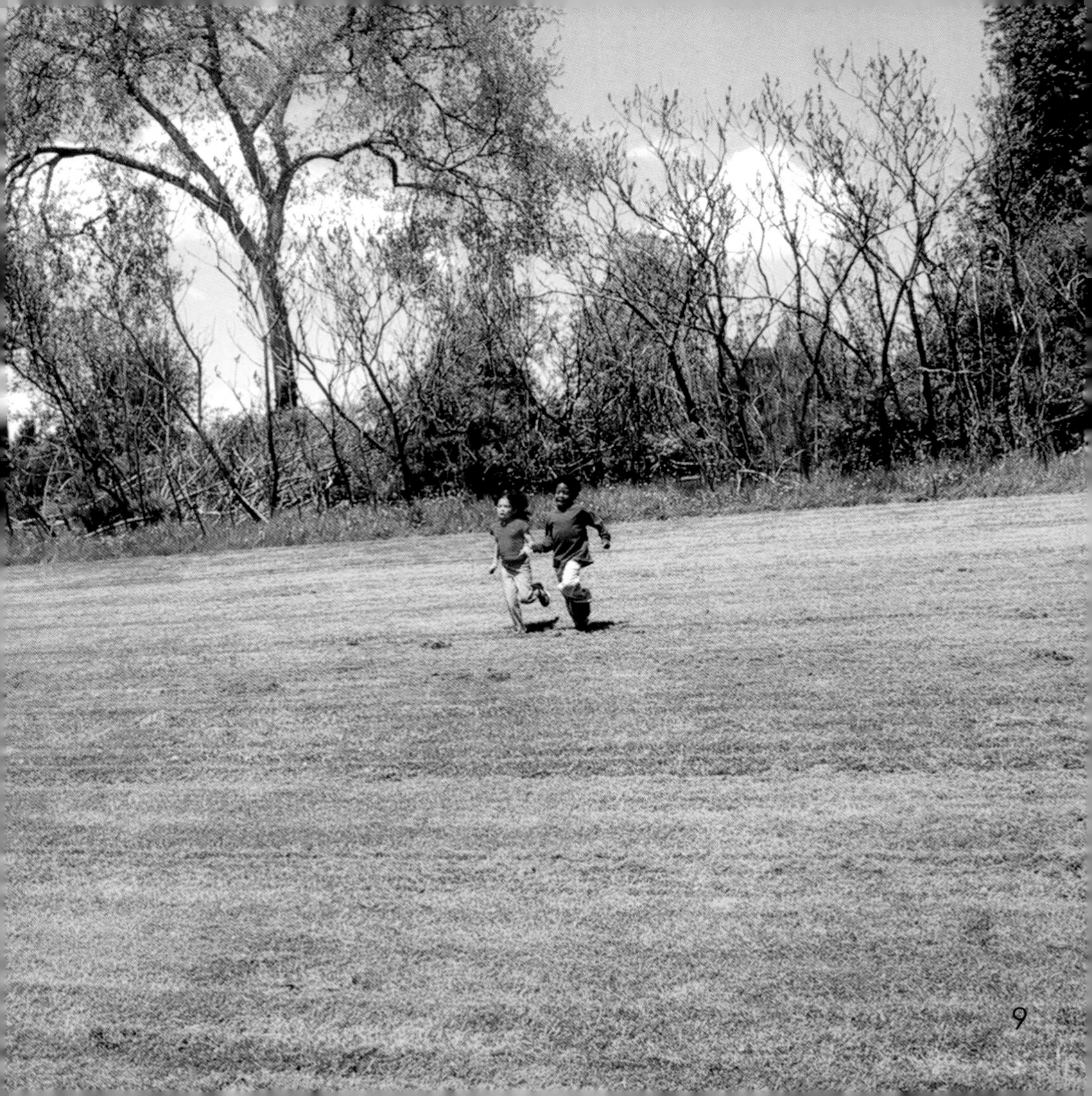

We like to play cards.

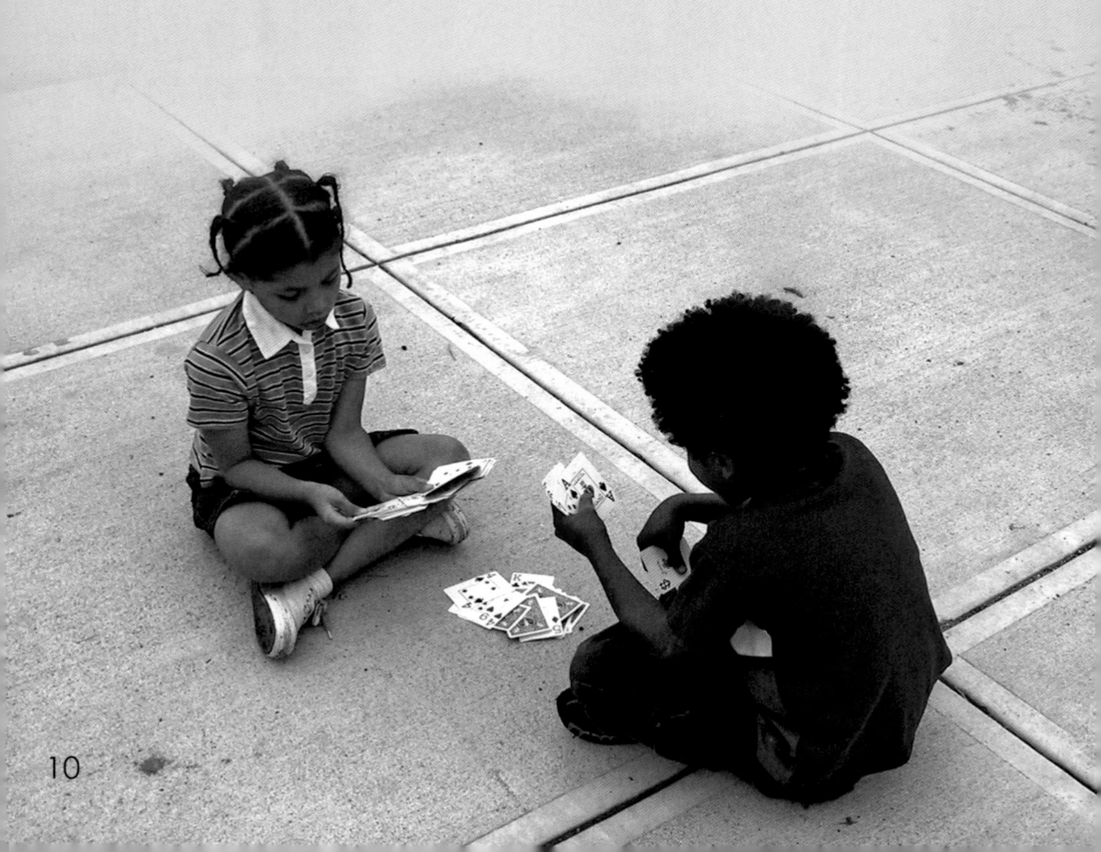

We like to read books.

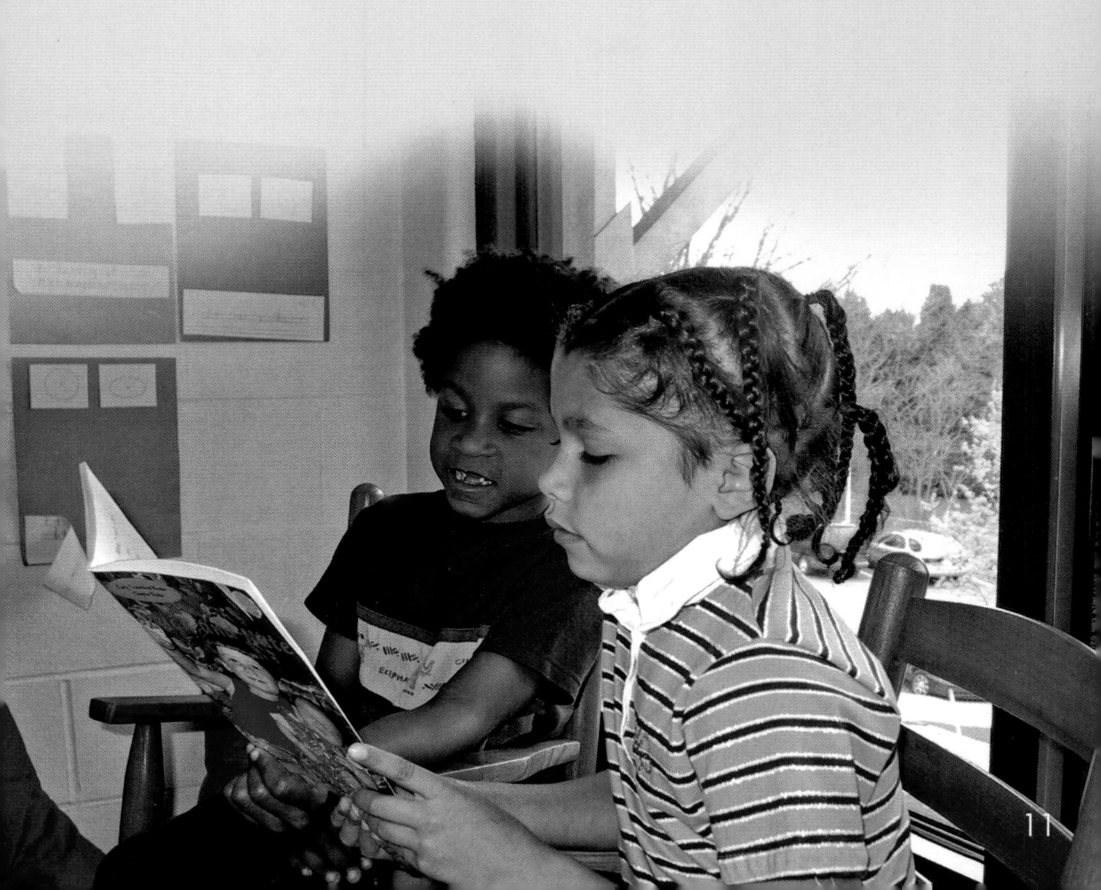

We like to play together.

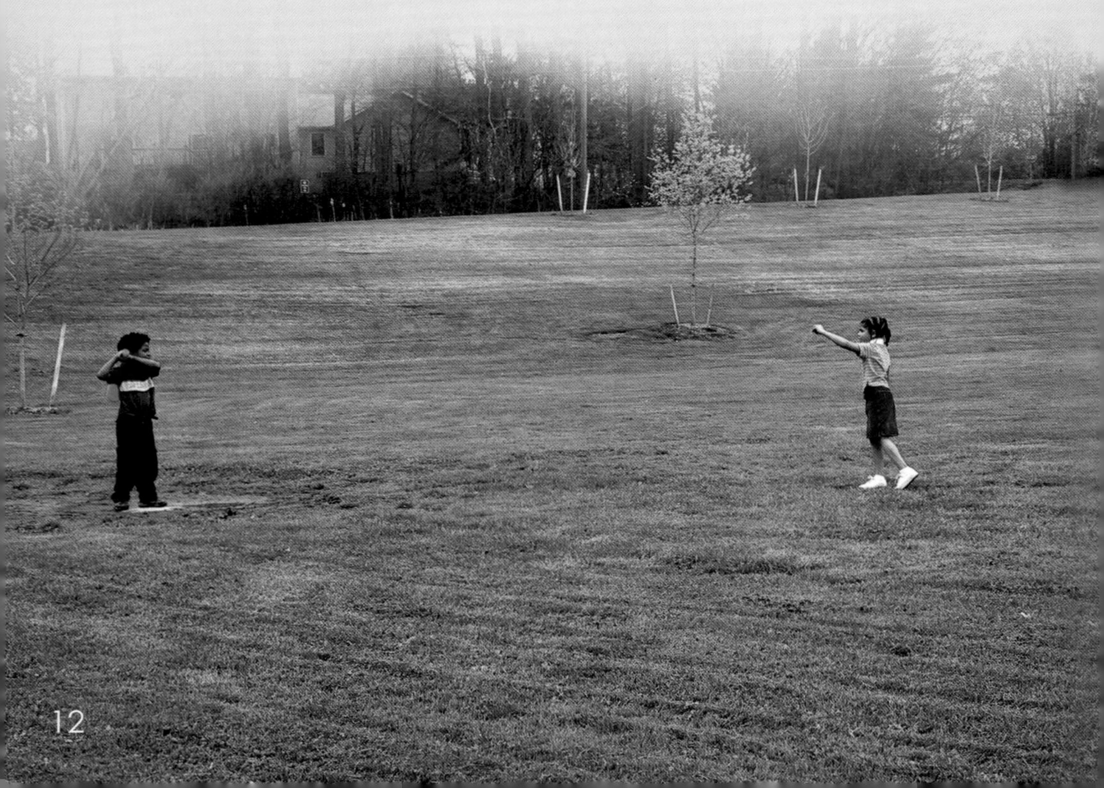